To my parents, Cyrena and Alan, who have supported me through everything I do.
To my fiancé Kirsty, who has been my rock, and my other friends and family,
who will always be there for me.

A CIP catalogue record for this title is available from the British Library.

ISBN 978 1 78612 173 8 (Paperback)
ISBN 978 1 78612 174 5 (Hardback)
ISBN 978 1 78612 175 2 (eBook)

www.austinmacauley.com

First Published (2016)
Austin Macauley Publishers Ltd.
25 Canada Square
Canary Wharf
London
E14 5LB

Alex has been working with children for seven years in schools and at activity camps.
He loves a wide range of sports, socialising, and being creative.
Alex has written poetry since his childhood.

Tilly the Tiger

Alex Weintroub

This is a story about
Tilly the tiger,
who really needed her
friends beside her.

One fine day in the blistering sun,
Tilly was rolling in the sand,
having some fun.
It was so, so hot on a perfect day,
she couldn't have wanted it any
other way.

As the day went on
Tilly wanted a drink,
but there was no
water around,
she needed to think.

The sun was so hot
that the water had gone,
but wait a minute,
something was wrong.

Tilly had never gone out of her home,
she'd lived there happily, all on her own.

As her journey began to find a lake,
she had no time to have a break.

Her first encounter was
Brian the bear,
she asked for his help,
in the hope that he'd care.

'Excuse me sir, I need something to drink, come and help me, what do you think?'

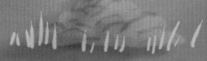

'I have nothing here but let's take a walk,
we can be friends and have a nice talk.'

Tilly had made her first new friend, 🌸
and Brian agreed to stay till the end.

Up ahead was Corey the croc,
who was lying down on his favourite rock.
'Excuse me sir, we need something to drink,
come and help us, what do you think?'

'Yes of course, I'm thirsty like you,
we must act fast, it's getting dark soon.'

Tilly now had made
two friends,
two that would stay
right till the end.

As they continued down the path,
knowing the evening was getting dark.
They met someone new,
he was small but keen,
hoping to know where the water had been.

Ollie the owl had a bird's eye view.
Where was the water? Surely he knew.
'Excuse me sir we need something to drink,
come and help us, what do you think?'

'I haven't seen any water for a while,
let's stick to the path, no more than a mile.'
Tilly and her friends were slowing down,
they had no energy, no water was around.
They came to a crossroads: 'Left or right?'
Nobody knew, no water in sight.

'Come with me, I know where to go,
I live in the lake,' said Hettie the hippo.
'If you all follow me, there's water this way,
come to my home, where we can all stay.'

Tilly and her friends
were happy to see
that the water was fresh
and clean as can be.
They drank, bathed,
played games and had fun,
because when friends stick together,
you're together as one.